Disney's
Winnie the Pooh
Loyal Through
and Through

The best friend in all the world

Is loyal and true-blue.

No matter what might come your way,

That friend will stand by you.

T he wind was very determined. But then, so was a little bear named Pooh.

"I've come to visit, Piglet!" Pooh shouted when he reached his friend's door. "The wind tried to stop me, but here I am!"

Piglet opened the door just enough to let Pooh come inside. But the wind yanked the door from Piglet's hand and threw it wide open! In blew leaves and twigs–and Pooh.

"Oh, dear," Piglet sighed. "This has been happening all day."

Pooh and Piglet pushed the door closed against the wind.
Pooh looked around at the mess in his friend's house.

"I've been sweeping and raking and chasing leaves for
hours," Piglet said. "And now I have to start all over again."

"I'll help you, Piglet," Pooh said. "Don't you worry. We'll have things cleaned up in no time."

"Oh, thank you," Piglet said gratefully. "You're a very good friend.

"I'll go get my broom and rake," Pooh said. "Then we can do twice the work in half the time . . . Or maybe it's half the work in twice the time. Oh, bother." Pooh headed back out into the wind. "Anyway, I'll be back soooooon!"

The wind pushed Pooh this way and that. He was very tired by the time he got to his house.

Pooh looked longingly at his cozy chair. "No," he said, collecting his broom and rake. "I said I would help Piglet, and I will."

It wasn't easy getting back to Piglet's house, but Pooh was determined to help his dear friend out.

"Oh, bother," Pooh said as he blew through his friend's door. "It sure is a windy kind of day."

There were leaves everywhere in Piglet's house. They were peeking out from under his table, piling up on top of his stove, and hiding in his cupboards. But together, Pooh and Piglet swept up every single one of them.

No sooner had Piglet and Pooh finished cleaning up the last leaf than Tigger came bouncing through Piglet's door, along with a gust of wind and more leaves.

"It's a splendiferous day for flying kites!" Tigger announced. "And I just happen to have a kite!"

Tigger smiled happily at Pooh and Piglet. "Come on! We can take turns flying it."

Piglet sadly shook his head. "You go ahead, Pooh," he said.
"I'll just stay and clean up. Again."

"It is kind of messy around here, isn't it, Buddy Boy?"
Tigger said.

"Are you coming, Pooh?" Tigger asked. "The wind's a-wasting."
Pooh looked sadly at Tigger's kite. Then he shook his head
firmly. "Thank you for asking, Tigger," he said. "But I'm going to
stay and help Piglet."

"Suit yourself," Tigger said. "Ta-ta for nowwwwwww," he added, bouncing back out into the wind.

As soon as Tigger was gone, Pooh and Piglet got back to work sweeping up the new leaves.

Pooh was under Piglet's table reaching for a leaf when they heard a knock. "Bother!" Pooh mumbled, as he sat up and hit his head. "Hello, Pooh and Piglet," Roo called from Piglet's doorway.

"I came to see if anyone wants to come sail my new sailboat with me," he said.

Pooh shook his sore head. "Sorry, Roo, but Piglet and I have some cleaning to do."

Just then Rabbit came blowing up to Piglet's door.
"Well," Rabbit said, doing his best to ignore the wind, "this
may not be the best day for collecting haycorns, but this is the
day I set aside to do it. Anyone care to join me?"

"I'm going to sail my boat, and Piglet is cleaning, and Pooh is helping Piglet because he said he would," Roo said in a rush.

"Oh. Well. I'm off, then," Rabbit said, letting go of the door.

"Me, toooooo," Roo called as he sailed out into the wind.

Alone again, Pooh and Piglet soon had Piglet's house leaf-free. "Now we can rake the leaves outside," Pooh said, holding the door open just a crack for Piglet to squeeze through. "And then we can go adventuring."

But the wind had other ideas. For every leaf that Pooh and Piglet captured, the wind blew two more into Piglet's yard. And then—just when the raking was almost done—an extra big gust of wind sent a shower of new leaves swirling down from the tree.

The sun was low in the sky and the wind was no longer
blowing when Pooh and Piglet finally finished raking.

"It's too late to go on any adventures now," Piglet said
sadly to Pooh.

"That's okay, Piglet. It was fun being here with you," Pooh said. "But I did get pretty tired of those leaves."

"Oh, me, too!" Piglet said. "But I am glad my house is no longer full of leaves. Thank you, Pooh."

At last the two tired friends sat down under the tree to rest.
Just then Tigger, Roo, and Rabbit all bounced into Piglet's yard.

"We want to celebrate what a loyal friend Pooh has been to you," Rabbit said to Piglet.

"Oh! Yes! That's a wonderful idea!" Piglet cried. "That would make me feel better about keeping Pooh from all the fun today."

"I stayed because I wanted to, Piglet," Pooh said. "You're my friend, and friends stick together—even on leaf-chasing days."

"That's why this is for you, Pooh," Rabbit said, holding a pot of honey with a tag that said, "To the Most Loyal Friend of All." Pooh smiled a tired, happy smile, and his friends all cheered, "Hooray for Pooh! He's loyal through and through!"

A LESSON A DAY POOH'S WAY

A loyal friend is someone

you can count on—

even when there's work to do!